OLIVIA™
and the Christmas Present

adapted by Farrah McDoogle

based on the screenplay "Olivia's Christmas Surprise" written by Scott Sonneborn

illustrated by Shane L. Johnson

Simon Spotlight

New York   London   Toronto   Sydney

Based on the TV series *OLIVIA*™ as seen on Nickelodeon™

SIMON SPOTLIGHT
An imprint of Simon & Schuster Children's Publishing Division
1230 Avenue of the Americas, New York, New York 10020
Copyright © 2011 Silver Lining Productions Limited (a Chorion company).
All rights reserved. OLIVIA™ and © 2011 Ian Falconer. All rights reserved.
All rights reserved, including the right of reproduction in whole or in part in any form.
SIMON SPOTLIGHT and colophon are registered trademarks of Simon & Schuster, Inc.
For information about special discounts for bulk purchases, please contact
Simon & Schuster Special Sales at 1-866-506-1949 or business@simonandschuster.com.
Manufactured in the United States of America 0811 LAK
First Edition 10 9 8 7 6 5 4 3 2 1
ISBN 978-1-4424-3624-4

This book belongs to:

_____

It was the night before Christmas, and Olivia had something very important and top secret to take care of. She crept quietly past her mom and dad, who were singing Christmas carols.

"Deck the halls with boughs of holly! Fa la la la la la la la la la," they sang.

Olivia quickly headed upstairs with Perry following not far behind.

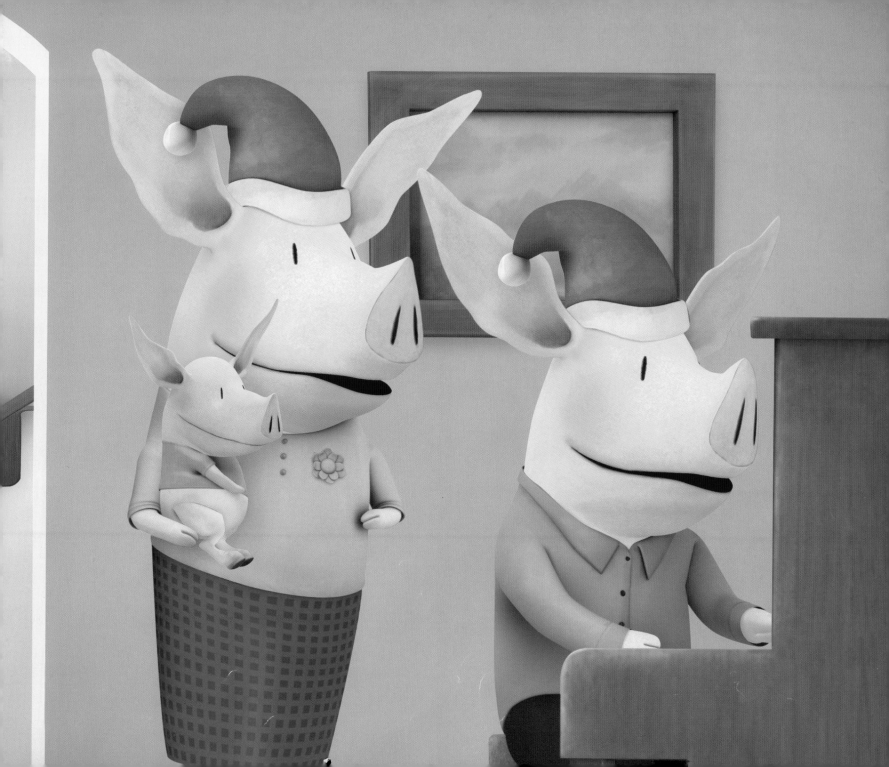

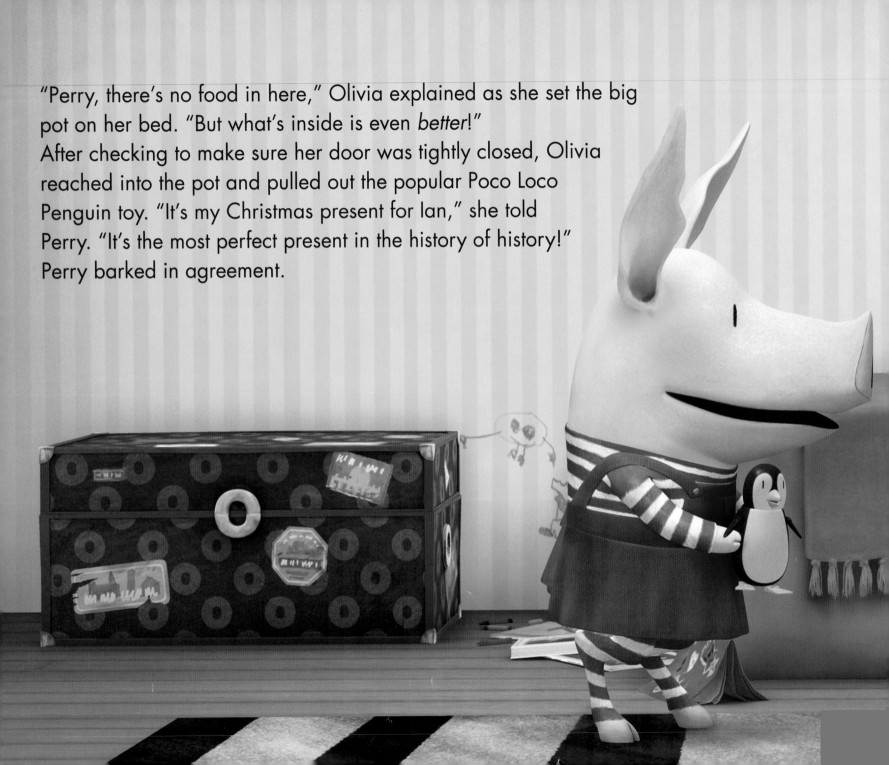

"Perry, there's no food in here," Olivia explained as she set the big pot on her bed. "But what's inside is even *better*!"
After checking to make sure her door was tightly closed, Olivia reached into the pot and pulled out the popular Poco Loco Penguin toy. "It's my Christmas present for Ian," she told Perry. "It's the most perfect present in the history of history!"
Perry barked in agreement.

"Now to wrap it," Olivia said as she rummaged through her trunk for some wrapping paper. "Perry, bark if you hear Ian coming!"

With the present perfectly wrapped, Olivia made a place for it under the Christmas tree. "Ian!" she cried as she spotted her brother hiding behind the tree, "Are you peeking at your presents?"

"No. Yes . . . maybe?" Ian replied.

"No peeking! You'll ruin the surprise!" Olivia exclaimed.

"But I'm such a good guesser!" Ian said.

Olivia knew Ian was right—he was the best present guesser she'd ever met. But Olivia also knew that she couldn't let Ian guess *this* present. It had to be kept a surprise!

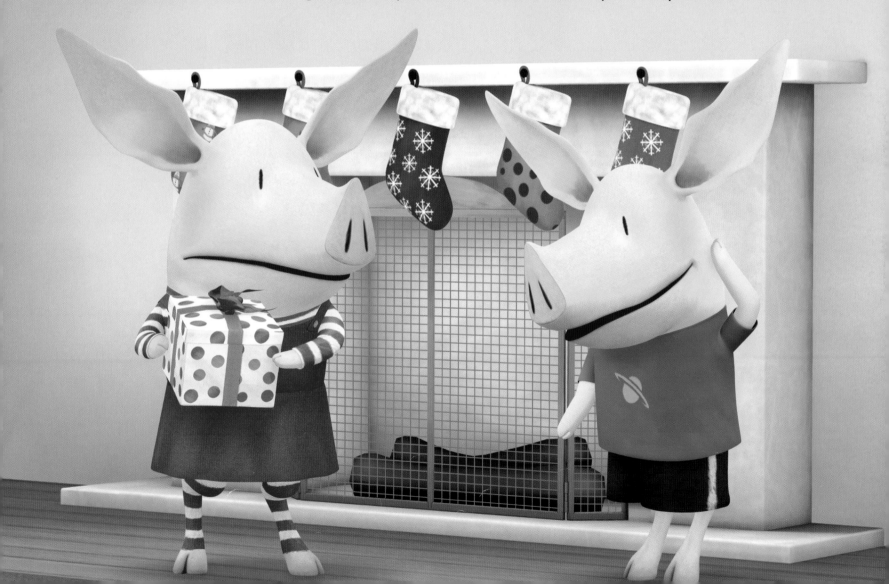

"What is it?" Ian asked as he lunged for the present. Olivia dashed away to her room and slammed the door before Ian could follow her in. After a moment Olivia slowly opened the door to check and see if the hallway was clear . . . and there was Ian!

"So what did you get me?" Ian insisted.

Olivia slammed her door again.

"I'm going to need a good hiding place for this present," Olivia said to herself. She decided to ask Francine for help. "Hey, Francine . . . ," she called out. Before Olivia could finish her sentence, Francine appeared at her side. "I need a good hiding place for Ian's present," Olivia finished.

"We should hide it in a place that Ian never goes," Francine suggested. Olivia smiled. She had the perfect place in mind.

"Ian's laundry," Olivia explained as she pointed to the hamper in the bathroom. "He never even goes near the dirty laundry hamper." "Problem solved!" Francine said.

Seconds later Mom came into the bathroom.
"Hi, girls," she said as she scooped up the
clothes from the hamper. "I'm just going
to run one more load of laundry before
Christmas."
"The present!" Olivia and Francine cried.

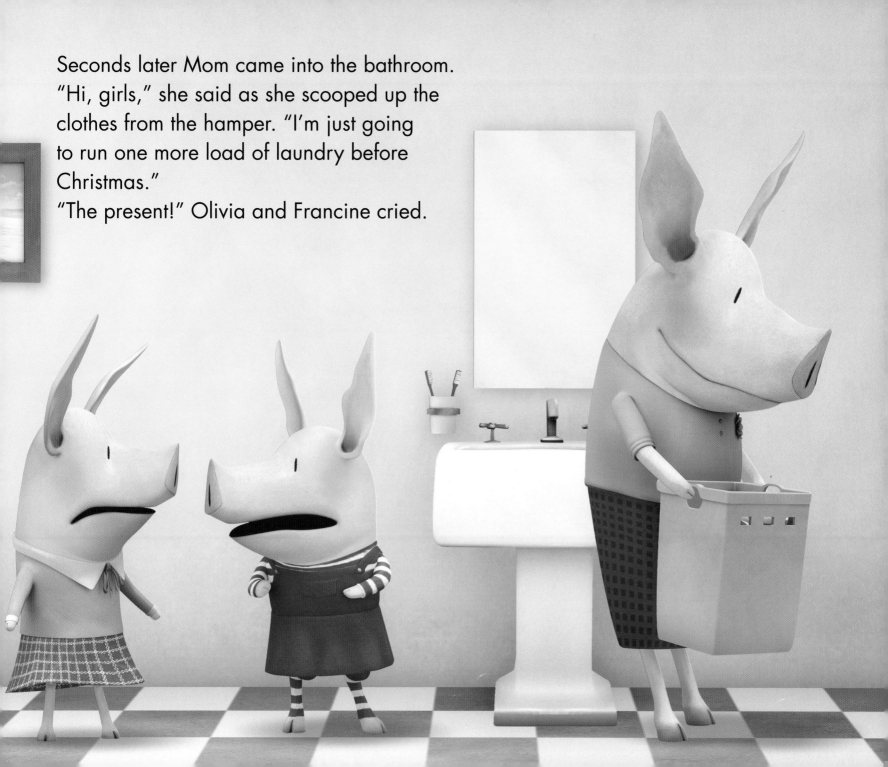

"That was close," Francine said.

The present safely back in her hands, Olivia tried to think of another hiding place.

"There's no safe place to hide this present inside the house," Francine said.

"You're right!" Olivia exclaimed. "There's just one thing to do . . . we'll go *outside*!"

Outside, Olivia and Francine found the perfect hiding place under a red bucket.

"No one will find the present here," Olivia said.

"Great! I'm going to go home now and hang my stocking," Francine said as she waved good-bye. "Merry Christmas, Olivia!"

"Merry Christmas, Francine," Olivia replied. "Thanks for your help!"

The next morning Olivia woke up thinking about one thing and one thing only.
"It's Christmas!" she cried, racing through the house to the backyard. "Time to get Ian's
Christmas . . . surprise?" Olivia gasped as she saw all the snow outside. "C'mon, Perry,"
she called as she grabbed a shovel. "We've got to dig to find Ian's present!"

Olivia and Perry began to dig, looking for the red bucket with Ian's gift. Perry found
something red . . . but it was just a bicycle.
"Keep digging!" Olivia instructed.
But it was no use . . . there was just so much snow.
"I'd have to be a machine to get rid of all this snow," Olivia said to herself. "I wonder . . ."

Olivia imagined what it would be like to be a flying robot with powerful jets of air coming out of her feet . . .

"Time for some super-duper snow blowing!" declares Olivia as she begins to clear the yard. "Ta-da!"

Olivia knew what to do.
She turned to Perry.
"Snow blower," she told him.

Soon Olivia had made her very own snow blower. Snow was flying everywhere. "It's working!" Olivia shouted.

Olivia pedaled harder and harder. *Whoosh!* The wind from Olivia's snow blower blew snow off the top of the red bucket. *Whoosh!* Another gust of wind tipped the red bucket over. "Ian's present!" Olivia cried happily.

Inside the house Ian was already looking at presents under the tree. "It's present time,"
Ian yelled when he saw Olivia.
"Merry Christmas, Ian," Olivia said as she handed him the present.
"I don't know how you did it, Olivia, but this is a surprise," said Ian.

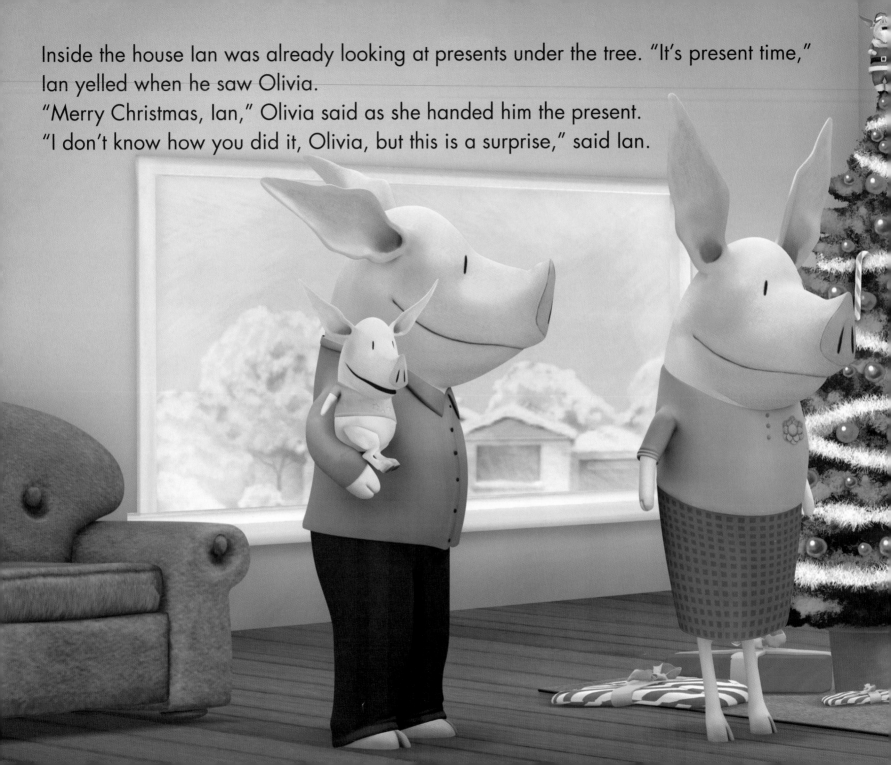

"Poco Loco Penguin!" Ian cried as he unwrapped his gift. "This is the best Christmas in the history of history!"

Ian gave Poco Loco Penguin a squeeze. "What is a skunk's favorite kind of sandwich?" it asked. "Peanut butter and smelly!"

Ian started laughing, and he gave his sister a big hug. Olivia beamed.

"So Santa did a good job this year?" Olivia's mom asked later that evening.

"The best!" Olivia replied. "I love all my presents! But my favorite gift was the one I surprised Ian with."

"I'm not surprised," Mother said. "It was a wonderful gift from a wonderful girl."

It was time for bed, but Olivia didn't want to go to sleep just yet.

"Good night, Olivia. And Merry Christmas . . ."

"Good night, Mom," said Olivia.